This book belongs to

_____

_____

To the brave children of the Canterbury earthquake
— and their pets.

When a disaster strikes, we all want to help. After the Christchurch earthquake, I thought, *If only I was a builder or a plumber, then I could be of some use to the people of Canterbury.* I wished I was an animal welfare officer, too, so that I could help find the lost and frightened cats that ran away from their homes when they sensed the earthquake was about to strike. But wishing is no good. Instead, the key to helping others is to use the skills we do have — whatever they may be.

   Thanks to the wonderful people at Scholastic New Zealand and to Christchurch's very own illustrator, Gavin Bishop, I've been able to use my skills as a writer to help out after the Christchurch earthquake.
—Diana Noonan

At first, I thought the wood pile behind our house had fallen. But as I rose from sleep, I remembered we didn't have a wood pile behind our house. My wife was already under the door frame. In a flash, I joined her. The roar that came from under the floor almost drowned out the sound of crashing and breaking. It was dark. I covered my head with my arms, waiting for the chimneys to crash through the ceiling. Finally Rūaumoko stopped. Tiny sounds from shattered glass and from timbers resettling tinkled through the black air.

   In Avonside, my daughter's house was trashed, split and broken. Her garden was filled with sand volcanoes. But a week later she got married. Together we all celebrated life amidst the enormous uncertainty that a major earthquake brings. My pictures in this book are for the children of Christchurch.

Thank you!

Following the major Canterbury earthquake of September 2010, *Quaky Cat* brought comfort and much-needed funds to Canterbury children and their families.
No one could ever have envisaged that, less than six months later, Christchurch would be struck again, this time by an even more devastating earthquake.

Now *Quaky Cat* is helping once more. Your purchase of this book will help support an even wider network of people affected by the earthquakes.

Scholastic New Zealand is donating to the Christchurch Mayoral Earthquake Appeal administered by the New Zealand Red Cross.

The author, Diana Noonan, is donating her royalties to the Christchurch Women's Refuge, www.womensrefuge.co.nz.

The illustrator, Gavin Bishop, is donating his royalties to Te Tai Tamariki: Aotearoa New Zealand Children's Literature Charitable Trust, www.tetaitamariki.org.nz.

And, in connection with the publication of this book, Scholastic Book Fairs and Book Clubs in the United States and Canada are donating $15,000 toward earthquake relief in New Zealand.

Scholastic New Zealand has gifted a copy of *Quaky Cat* to each of the 15,000 year 1 and 2 children in the affected area.

Diana Noonan | Gavin Bishop

Quaky Cat

SCHOLASTIC INC.
New York Toronto London Auckland
Sydney Mexico City New Delhi Hong Kong

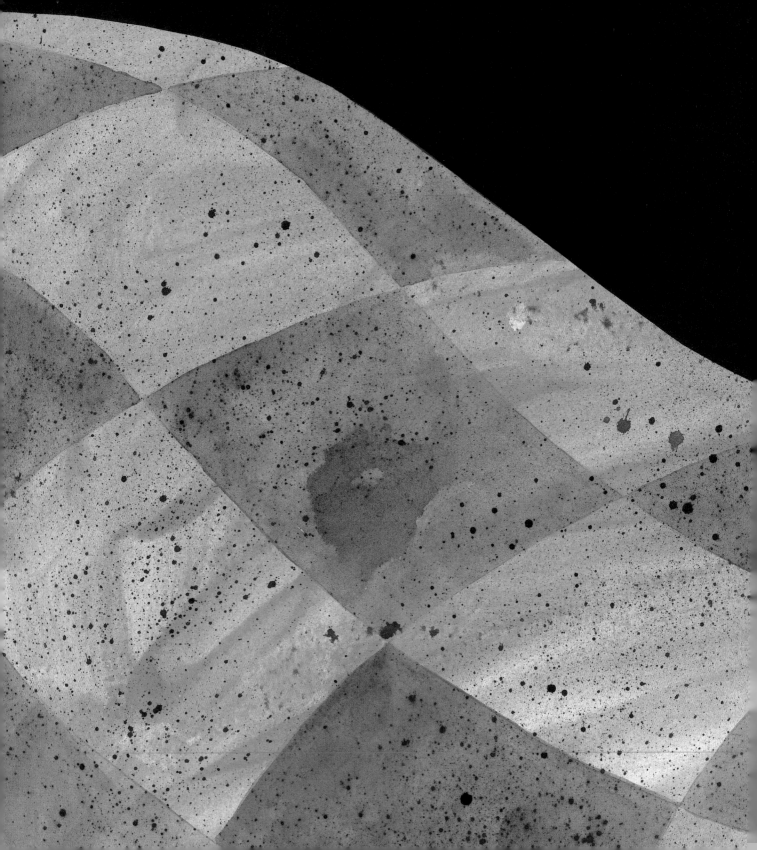

On a cold Christchurch morning, while the city was sleeping,
before the birds roused him with twitters and cheeping,
curled up on the end of his friend Emma's bed,
Tiger woke with a start ... and a feeling of dread.

He twitched his long whiskers and sniffed at the air.
Danger was close, but what was it — and where?
Then a voice in his head, one he'd not heard before,
shouted, *Run for your life, Tiger! Make for the door!*

Tiger fled from the house with a leap and a bound
as, louder than thunder, from deep underground,
came a roar and a shudder and terrible shaking!
Around him, the city was rolling and quaking.

He raced up the path as it buckled and bent,
as the mailbox swayed — even faster he went!
'Round swings that were squeaking and merry-go-rounds creaking,
past the shuddering school with its swimming pool leaking.

Over the river on bridges that wiggled,
he shot through the city on sidewalks that jiggled.
Above him, the pigeons fled tumbling perches
and dodged 'round the spires of crumbling churches.

The whole city rocked. It reeled and it rolled.
All by themselves the cathedral bells tolled.
With no place to hide and no time to spare,
Tiger shot up a quivering tree in the square.

When he'd clawed his way up to the top, he looked down ...
and saw, in the tree, half the cats from the town!
Below them bricks crashed, chimneys fell, shops caved in.
Sirens were wailing — and the cats joined the din.

As the sun rose that morning, the world looked with pity
at the folks on the streets of their tumbled-down city.
In the tree, Tiger shivered, he was cold and forlorn.
Where was his Emma, in this muddled-up dawn?

Afraid, the cats huddled, with hisses and wails,
with whiskers cast down and sad, drooping tails,
till evening, when one puss came down on his own
and set out through the rubble to look for his home.

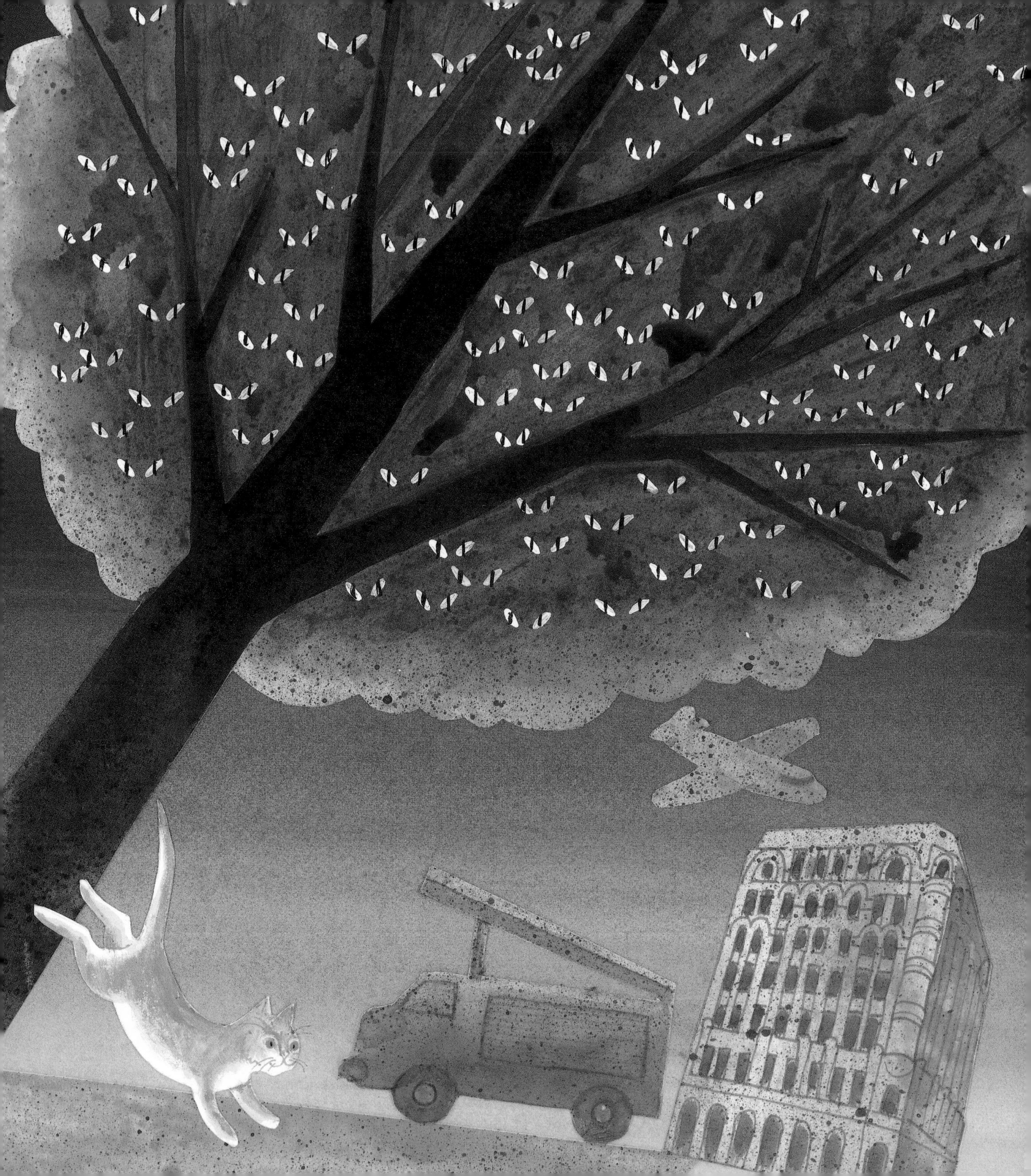

as he passed perchless pigeons puffed up with the cold,
and crossed broken bridges pushed up into humps,
the school pool now empty, the field full of lumps.

Over the merry-go-rounds, not fit to ride,
he padded past tangles of swings on their sides.

At last, to his street he came, weary and worn —
but where was his mailbox? Where was his lawn?

Gone was the place that Tiger called home,
and gone was his Emma. He felt so alone.
Where could he go and what should he do?
He was tired, he was hungry — but then he smelled stew!

He sniffed his way down to the end of the street,
and into a hall through a tangle of feet.

People were gathering, their plates piled high,
Would they give him a morsel — one small bite to try?
Poor Tiger-puss waited ... didn't anyone care?
Then everything changed with the cry, "Look who's here!"

It was Emma! His Emma! He was back home at last,
and his horrible day was a thing of the past.
His house was in ruins, the whole city battered,
but with Emma's arms 'round him, none of it mattered.

For a home's not a roof, or a chimney or stairs,
it isn't a cat door or tables and chairs.
Home's not a mailbox, home's not a floor,
a home isn't gone with a quake and a roar.

Home is a pat and a scratch 'round the ears,
home is a rest from the noise and the fears,
home is a family, home is a hug,
home is a friend and a neighbor's warm rug.

Home is the giving and helping and sharing.
When a city is crumbling, then home is the caring.
Home is a lap where it's cozy and warm ...
home is where love keeps you safe from the storm.

Glossary

Some people find earthquakes scary. Others think they're fascinating. However you feel about earthquakes, they *are* very interesting, so it's good to have some words to help you talk about them. Here are just a few:

aftershocks	The earthquakes felt in the days, weeks, and months after a main earthquake.
jolt	A sudden movement.
liquefaction	This is when an earthquake jiggles soil so much that it's not strong enough to hold up buildings anymore. Liquefaction can make houses sink down into the ground or end up on a lean.
plates	These are gigantic areas of deep-underground rock, bigger than countries (they're sometimes called *tectonic* plates). Plates move very, very slowly, but sometimes we feel the movement as an earthquake.
Richter scale	A way of describing how strong an earthquake is. (The September 4, 2010, Canterbury earthquake was very strong. It measured 7.1 on the Richter scale.)
Rūaumoko	The Māori word for "earthquake god." Rūaumoko was also the youngest child of Rangi-nui (the Sky Father) and Papa-tū-ā-nuku (the Earth Mother).
seismograph	A machine that measures underground movements such as earthquakes.
seismologist	A scientist who studies underground movements such as earthquakes.
shaking	The wobbly feeling we notice during an earthquake. Other words to describe this feeling are: *tremors*, *quaking*, *vibrating*, and *quivering*.
uplift	Ground that has been pushed up by plates as they move deep under the earth. In an earthquake, ground can be uplifted very suddenly.

As a cat lover I was intrigued by Tiger's adventure, and my wife, Jo, and I saw a little bit of our own three cats in Tiger. When the quake struck in the early hours of Saturday, September 4, our oldest cat, Blue, bolted. Although he was somewhere in our warehouse home, our scaredy cat didn't reappear for several days. How different to our unflappable Ringo, who just rolled over and went back to sleep. Cuddly little Quasar, a baldie sphinx, was downstairs with Jo and true to his timid nature snuggled in extra tight until the shaking was over. They would all agree with Tiger's description of home — *a place where love keeps you safe from the storm.*

Thank you to all those involved in the publication of *Quaky Cat* — its talented author Diana Noonan and Christchurch illustrator Gavin Bishop, who both worked for long hours for free, and Scholastic New Zealand for generously donating half the proceeds to Canterbury charities. This is a book our very brave children (and adults) will treasure.

—Bob Parker, Mayor of Christchurch

Waking in the morning — it is almost half-past four —
the windows rattle wildly! Yes! The wolf is at the door!
My gliding and colliding books leap freely into space,
and all the things that seemed secure are quickly changing place.
As our foundations tremble and the city starts to groan,
we feel the flick of board and brick ... the impotence of stone.
The earth reminds us what we are — mere fleas that crawl its hide ...
It battles — rattles chattels as our noble buildings slide.
We went to bed as masters, but we feel the city sprawl
and leap awake, remembering how far we have to fall.

—Margaret Mahy

Much like Quaky Cat, my family and I were woken with a fright on the night of September 4th and ran for the door with our tails between our legs. It sounded like a jumbo jet was landing in our backyard and we all felt like a pair of rolled up socks inside a washing machine on the spin cycle!

I will always remember the great fear of the unknown: when will this stop, will life ever be the same again — and, incredibly, how as a family and as a city we came together and helped each other through.

We have two cats, a pig, two piglets, a dog, twenty chickens, and a rooster! We'll never know what they were thinking as they were woken with a shudder that night, falling off perches, rolling over the hay, and being shocked out of their comfy beds. *Quaky Cat* is a wonderful insight into what may have been going through the minds of animals all over Christchurch. Pet owners everywhere will be captivated by this truly heartwarming tale.

—Jason Gunn

First published in 2010 by Scholastic New Zealand Limited

ISBN 978-0-545-38765-1

12 11 10 9 8 7 6 5 4 3 2 1   11 12 13 14 15 16/0

Printed in the U.S.A.   08

This edition first printing, April 2011

Original publishing team: Diana Murray, Penny Scown, and Annette Bisman
Design: Book Design Ltd, www.bookdesign.co.nz